This Book Belongs To:

_____

For Rosa, who made the suggestion;
For Geoffrey, who thought it was a good idea;
For Frank and Joyce, who believed
in it;
And for Brian, who saw that it got done;

and

For Auntie Tachiko, who introduced
me to Manapua.

This is a Brand-New Book, Written and Illustrated
Especially for Polychrome Books

All characters in this book are fictitious, and any resemblance to actual persons living or
dead is purely coincidental.

ISBN NO. 1-879965-00-3

Char Siu Bao Boy

Written by Sandra S. Yamate
Illustrated by Joyce M.W. Jenkin

Charlie liked char siu bao.

He liked it better than candy.
He liked it better than cookies.

He liked it better than pizza.
It was his FAVORITE food.

Charlie liked char siu bao steamed.
He liked it baked.
He even liked it COLD.

Sometimes, Charlie helped Grandmother make char siu bao. He helped her bake the bright red barbequed pork that was the char siu.

He helped her roll the fluffy dough that would be wrapped around the char siu.

He helped her shape them into nice round balls. Best of all, Charlie helped sample each batch of char siu bao...

... just to make sure it tasted
DELICIOUS!

Every day when Charlie went to school, he carried his lunch.

And every day for lunch he brought char siu bao.

All of the other boys and girls made faces when
Charlie ate his char siu bao.

"UGH!" said the boys.

"YECH!" said the girls.

"Why can't you eat a sandwich like everyone else?"
asked his best friend Mike.

"Char siu bao is like a sandwich," explained Charlie.
"It's a Chinese sandwich."

It didn't matter.
All the other boys and girls thought char siu bao
looked TERRIBLE.

So, Charlie tried to eat other things for lunch.
One day he brought a peanut butter sandwich.
Another day he brought a hot dog.

Still another day he brought a ham sandwich, and
then egg salad.

Before long he had tried tuna salad, turkey and even salami sandwiches.

"Aren't they good?" asked the other boys and girls.

Charlie didn't say anything. He missed his delicious char siu bao.

Then one day Charlie had an idea.

He whispered his idea to Grandmother.
She smiled and nodded.

The next day at lunchtime each boy and girl found a char siu bao in front of them.

"I've tried to eat sandwiches that you like," said Charlie. "Now it's your turn to try the char siu bao that I like. It's not fair for you to make faces at it until you've tried it."

The boys and girls looked at each other.

It was true. None of them had ever tried char siu bao before. They looked at the char siu bao.

Some SNIFFED at it.

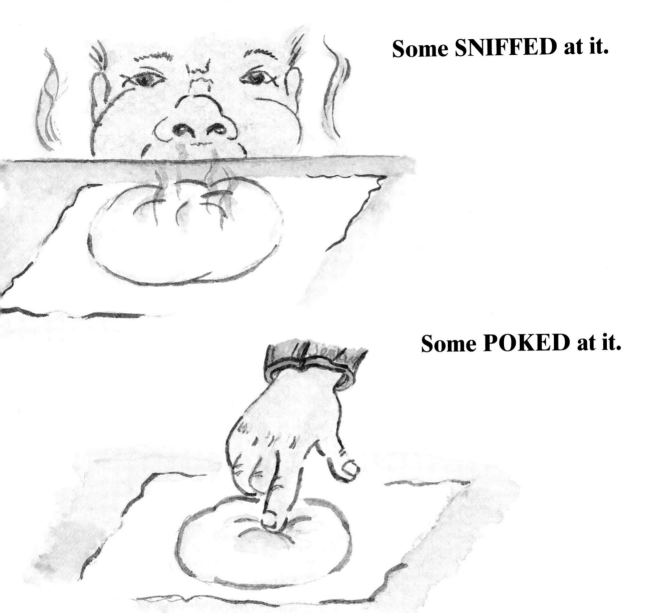

Some POKED at it.

Charlie wondered if anyone would try a piece of char siu bao.

Finally, his best friend Mike looked at him and sighed.

Mike picked up the char siu bao. He took a deep breath.

Everyone was silent, watching Mike.

Mike bit into the char siu bao. He chewed, he swallowed ...

... and he smiled.

"HEY, this is GOOD!" exclaimed Mike.

The other boys and girls each picked up their char siu bao.

Some took BIG bites.

Some took little bites.

Before long, EVERYONE was eating char siu bao!

"This char siu bao IS delicious! We're glad we tried it!" they said. "Thank you, Charlie."

Charlie smiled. "You're welcome," he said. "I'm happy to share my favorite food with all my friends."

Now, Charlie still brings char siu bao for lunch every day.

But he also brings extras to share with all his friends.

THE END

To order more copies of this or other titles from Polychrome Publishing Corporation or if you wish to be on our mailing list, please write to:

Polychrome Publishing Corporation
4509 North Francisco Avenue
Chicago, Illinois 60625-3808

or call:
1.312. 478-4455
or fax:
1.312. 478-0786

ATTENTION Writers and Storytellers!
Polychrome Publishing is interested in you!

For more information, call or write to the attention of our Editorial Department.